# The Bear's Cave

by Regine Schindler
illustrated by Sita Jucker

DUTTON CHILDREN'S BOOKS  •  NEW YORK

One chilly autumn day, Rabbit and Mouse were talking in a field.

"Rabbit, how do you stay warm in winter?" Mouse asked.

Rabbit looked up at the sky. He wanted to impress Mouse. "I fly south with the birds," he said.

"Are those your wings?" Mouse pointed to Rabbit's ears.

"Yes," said Rabbit. "Aren't they wonderfully long?" He gave them a wiggle.

Mouse thought for a moment. "I fly south with the birds, too."

"Surely *you* don't have wings," Rabbit scoffed.

"Oh, yes I do!" replied Mouse. "Only one, but it's very long, indeed." And she waved her tail.

That afternoon, the sky grew dark early.

"It smells like snow," said Mouse softly.

"I know," said Rabbit. "Let's find a warm place to hide."

Rabbit and Mouse burrowed in a bed of leaves by the side of the road. Overhead the birds flew south.

Soon the air was filled with whirling snowflakes. By morning, a white blanket had covered the earth.

Mouse poked her head up through the bed of leaves, up through the blanket of snow. *Cold, white, wet*, she thought. *I need a cave.*

But to Rabbit she said, "We're lucky we can fly south with the birds."

Rabbit agreed. "And it's time to get going. But we'll have to split up. I fly better when no one is watching me."

"That's all right," said Mouse. "So do I."

"See you in the South!" said Rabbit. He bounded away.

Poor Mouse struggled through the snow, trying to think where she could find a nice, warm cave. Suddenly she saw some tracks. *Rabbit tracks!* she thought. *I wonder if Rabbit's still here!*

The tracks led up and up, to a deep dark hole in the side of a cliff. *That looks like a bear's cave,* she thought. *Surely Rabbit's not in there.* Mouse looked around. She saw something moving.

It was Rabbit, shivering on a ledge.

"Rabbit!"

"Mouse!"

"I thought you were in the South with the birds," Mouse called.

For a moment, Rabbit didn't say anything. Then he called down, "I just came back too soon. What about you? Didn't you fly south?"

"Yes, indeed," Mouse said. "Only I left early, too."

"Pity," said Rabbit. "Anyway, I was thinking of dropping in on Bear before he goes to sleep. Would you like to join me? I'll bet his cave is nice and warm."

Rabbit and Mouse tiptoed up to the mouth of the cave. Very carefully, they poked their heads in.

Bear sat up.

"Well, well, well," he grumbled in his great, deep voice. "Who dares to disturb me and my winter's sleep?"

"We beg your pardon, sir," said Rabbit hastily. "It's just Mouse and me. We hoped you might let us come in for a little while."

"This is my cave, my bear's cave, for me alone," growled Bear. "It's not a home for frozen ragamuffins."

"Perhaps you'd like a bedtime story," suggested Mouse. "We could tell you about our trip. We flew south with the birds."

Now, Bear found this of interest. He had been having trouble falling asleep, and a good bedtime story might be just the thing.

Rabbit and Mouse began to tell Bear everything they could think of about their trip south. They told him about palm trees and spikey cacti and about wrinkly elephants and striped zebras. They told him about fat hippos and pink flamingos. As they talked, they stole closer and closer to Bear until they were snuggled right into his big, soft shoulders.

Soon Bear was fast asleep.

All winter long, Rabbit and Mouse stayed warm in Bear's cave. Whenever Bear tossed and turned and seemed to be waking, they whispered more stories about wrinkly elephants and striped zebras, fat hippos and pink flamingos.

And Bear would fall back to sleep.

As the days got warmer, Bear woke more and more often. Finally, when the trees were dripping and the air smelled of fresh earth, Bear stepped out into the sunlight. He wobbled around on his sleepy legs and felt the soft mud squish between his toes. Then he lumbered back to his cave.

"It is spring," boomed Bear.

Mouse and Rabbit were hungry and anxious to leave. "Thank you, Bear, for sharing your cave. You kept us safe and cozy."

"Thank *you*," replied Bear, "for sharing your stories. I've never had such a good nap. I do hope you'll visit me next winter. But before you go—there is one thing. Won't you show me your wings? I'd love to see you fly."

"Certainly, certainly," Rabbit assured him. "We'd be glad to fly for you. But since we haven't used our wings all winter, we'll need a big running start. You wait here."

Quick as a flash, Rabbit and Mouse were out of the cave.

"Tell the truth, my dear friend," said Rabbit as they raced along. "Your stories were wonderful. But your tail isn't really a wing, is it?"

"And you, dear Rabbit," panted Mouse, trying to keep up. "You don't really have wings in your ears, do you?"

Rabbit laughed. "No, but I do have the quickest legs of all the animals. Watch this!" And with a great kick he bounded out of sight.

Bear waited and waited, watching the sky. After a while, he grew impatient. And suspicious. "Those pipsqueaks," he grumbled. "I'm going to look for them."

Bear crashed off into the forest. He traveled down one path after another, bellowing, "Rabbit! Mouse! Answer me! It's me! Bear!"

Finally, between the trees, he caught a glimpse of Rabbit bounding through the bushes. He saw Mouse, darting from rock to rock.

"Wings, ha!" cried Bear. "I get it now. They never flew south with the birds. They never flew anywhere. They made their stories up! Still...they were good stories."

Bear growled to himself and thought a bit. "I bet I could make up stories, too."

"I flew south with the birds," roared Bear, in his great Bear voice, to all the plants and animals in the forest. "Here are my mighty wings." He held up his paws and wiggled his long, sharp claws. And then he told his stories his own way. "I saw palm cacti and spikey trees. I saw wrinkled zebras and striped elephants. I saw fat flamingos and pink hippos. I saw everything there is to see—I saw it all."

Over and over, all summer long, Bear told his stories of the South to anyone who would listen.

And when the air grew cold and the sky darkened early, he started to return to his cave. He looked forward to seeing Rabbit and Mouse again, and to the stories they would tell.

Bear wondered where they would all fly this winter.

Copyright © 1988 by bohem press

Translated by Christopher Franceschelli
Translation copyright © 1989 by Dutton Children's Books

All rights reserved.

First published in the United States in 1990 by
Dutton Children's Books,
a division of Penguin Books USA Inc.

Originally published in Switzerland in 1988 by
bohem press—Zurich, Recklinghausen. Wien
under the title *Die Bärenhöhle*.

First American Edition
Printed in Hong Kong by South China Printing Co.
10 9 8 7 6 5 4 3 2 1

*Library of Congress Cataloging-in-Publication Data*
Schindler, Regine.
    [Bärenhöhle. English]
    The bear's cave/by Regine Schindler; illustrated by Sita
Jucker.—1st American ed.
        p.   cm.
    Translation of: Die Bärenhöhle.
    Summary: Rabbit and Mouse spend the winter with Bear in his cave,
telling him wonderful but untrue stories of how they can fly and the
things they have seen.
    ISBN 0-525-44553-6
    [1. Rabbits—Fiction.   2. Mice—Fiction.   3. Bears—Fiction.
4. Winter—Fiction.   5. Storytelling—Fiction.]   I. Jucker, Sita,
ill.   II. Title.                                          90-30273
PZ7.S34635Be   1990                                           CIP
[E]—dc20                                                        AC